S0-CNJ-035

WALT DISNEY PRESENTS

Winnie-the-Pooh
AND TIGGER

A STORY BY A. A. MILNE

Pictures by
THE WALT DISNEY STUDIO

gb

GOLDEN PRESS
Western Publishing Company, Inc.
Racine, Wisconsin

...tle Golden Book was produced under the supervision of

THE WALT DISNEY STUDIO

Fourteenth Printing, 1977

Text in this book Copyright, 1928, by E. P. Dutton & Co., Inc. Copyright Renewal, © 1956 by A. A. Milne. Illustrations in this book Copyright © 1968, 1964 by Walt Disney Productions. All rights reserved. Material in this volume is derived from THE HOUSE AT POOH CORNER written by A. A. Milne with illustrations by E. H. Shepard and published by E. P. Dutton & Co., Inc. Produced in the U.S.A. by Western Publishing Company, Inc.

GOLDEN, A LITTLE GOLDEN BOOK®, and GOLDEN PRESS®
are trademarks of Western Publishing Company, Inc. No part of this
book may be reproduced or copied in any form without written per-
mission from the publisher.

Now it happened that Kanga had felt rather motherly that morning, and Wanting to Count Things—like Roo's vests, and how many pieces of soap there were left, and the two clean spots in Tigger's feeder; so she had sent them out with a packet of watercress sandwiches for Roo and a packet of extract-of-malt sandwiches for Tigger, to have a nice long morning in the Forest not getting into mischief. And off they had gone.

And as they went, Tigger told Roo (who wanted to know) all about the things that Tiggers could do.

"Can they fly?" asked Roo.

"Yes," said Tigger, "they're very good flyers, Tiggers are, Stornry good flyers."

"Oo!" said Roo. "Can they fly as well as Owl?"

"Yes," said Tigger. "Only they don't want to."

"Why don't they want to?"

"Well, they just don't like it, somehow."

Roo couldn't understand this, because he thought it would be lovely to be able to fly, but Tigger said it was difficult to explain to anybody who wasn't a Tigger himself.

"Well," said Roo, "can they jump as far as Kangas?"

"Yes," said Tigger. "When they want to."

"I *love* jumping," said Roo. "Let's see who can jump farthest, you or me."

"*I* can," said Tigger. "But we mustn't stop now, or we shall be late."

"Late for what?"

"For whatever we want to be in time for," said Tigger, hurrying on.

In a little while they came to the Six Pine Trees.

"I can swim," said Roo. "I fell into the river, and I swimmed. Can Tiggers swim?"

"Of course they can. Tiggers can do everything."

"Can they climb trees better than Pooh?" asked Roo, stopping under the tallest Pine Tree, and looking up at it.

"Climbing trees is what they do best," said Tigger. "Much better than Poohs."

"Could they climb this one?"

"They're always climbing trees like that," said Tigger. "Up and down all day."

"Oo, Tigger, are they *really*?"

"I'll show you," said Tigger bravely, "and you can sit on my back and watch me." For of all the things which he had said Tiggers could do, the only one he felt really certain about suddenly was climbing trees.

"Oo, Tigger, oo, Tigger, oo, Tigger!" squeaked Roo excitedly.

So he sat on Tigger's back and up they went.

And for the first ten feet Tigger said happily to himself, "Up we go!"

And for the next ten feet he said:

"I always *said* Tiggers could climb trees."

And for the next ten feet he said:

"Not that it's easy, mind you."

And for the next ten feet he said:

"Of course, there's the coming-down too. Backwards."

And then he said:
"Which will be difficult . . ."

"Unless one fell . . ."
"when it would be . . ."

"EASY."

And at the word "easy" the branch he was standing on broke suddenly, and he just managed to clutch at the one above him as he felt himself going . . .

. . . and then slowly he got his chin over it . . . and then one back paw . . . and then the other . . . until at last he was sitting on it, breathing very quickly, and wishing that he had gone in for swimming instead.

Roo climbed off, and sat down next to him.

"Oo, Tigger," he said excitedly, "are we at the top?"

"No," said Tigger.

"Are we going to the top?"

"No," said Tigger.

"Oh," said Roo rather sadly. And then he went on hopefully: "That was a lovely bit just now, when you pretended we were going to fall-bump-to-the-bottom, and we didn't. Will you do that bit again?"

"NO," said Tigger.

Roo was silent for a little while, and then he said, "Shall we eat our sandwiches, Tigger?" And Tigger said, "Yes, where are they?" And Roo said, "At the bottom of the tree." And Tigger said, "I don't think we'd better eat them just yet." So they didn't.

By and by Pooh and Piglet came along.

"Look, Pooh!" said Piglet suddenly. "There's something in one of the Pine Trees."

"So there is!" said Pooh, looking up wonderingly. "There's an Animal."

"Pooh!" cried Piglet. "I believe it's Tigger and Roo!"

"So it is," said Pooh.

"Hallo, Roo!" called Piglet. "What are you doing?"

"We can't get down, we can't get down!" cried Roo. "Isn't it fun? Pooh, isn't it fun, Tigger and I are living in a tree, like Owl, and we're going to stay here for ever and ever. I can see Piglet's house. Piglet, I can see your house from here. Aren't we high? Is Owl's house as high up as this?"

"How did you get there, Roo?" asked Piglet.

"On Tigger's back! And Tiggers can't climb downwards, because their tails get in the way, only upwards, and Tigger forgot about that when we started, and he's only just remembered. So we've got to stay here for ever and ever—unless we go higher. What did you say, Tigger? Oh, Tigger says if we go higher we shan't be able to see Piglet's house so well, so we're going to stop here."

"Piglet," said Pooh solemnly, when he had heard all this, "what shall we do?" And he began to eat Tigger's sandwiches.

"Are they stuck?" asked Piglet anxiously.

Pooh nodded.

"Couldn't you climb up to them?"

"I might, Piglet, and I might bring Roo down on my back, but I couldn't bring Tigger down. So we must think of something else." And in a thoughtful way he began to eat Roo's sandwiches, too.

Whether he would have thought of anything before he had finished the last sandwich, I don't know, but he had just got to the last but one when there was a crackling in the bracken, and Christopher Robin and Eeyore came strolling along together.

"I shouldn't be surprised if it hailed a good deal tomorrow," Eeyore was saying. "Blizzards and whatnot. Being fine today doesn't Mean Anything. It has no sig—what's that word? Well, it has none of that. It's just a small piece of weather."

"There's Pooh!" said Christopher Robin, who didn't much mind *what* it did tomorrow, as long as he was out in it. "Hallo, Pooh!"

"It's Christopher Robin!" said Piglet. "*He'll* know what to do."
They hurried up to him.

"Oh, Christopher Robin," began Pooh.

"And Eeyore," said Eeyore.

"Tigger and Roo are right up the Six Pine Trees, and they
can't get down, and——"

"And I was just saying," put in Piglet, "that if only Christopher
Robin——"

"*And* Eeyore——"

"If only you were here, then we could think of something to do."

Christopher Robin looked up at Tigger and Roo, and tried to
think of something.

"*I* thought," said Piglet earnestly, "that if Eeyore stood at the bottom of the tree, and if Pooh stood on Eeyore's back, and if I stood on Pooh's shoulders——"

"And if Eeyore's back snapped suddenly, then we could all laugh. Ha ha! Amusing in a quiet way," said Eeyore, "but not really helpful."

"Well," said Piglet meekly, "*I* thought——"

"Would it break your back, Eeyore?" asked Pooh, very much surprised.

"That's what would be so interesting, Pooh. Not being quite sure till afterwards."

Pooh said "Oh!" and they all began to think again.

"I've got an idea!" cried Christopher Robin suddenly.

"Listen to this, Piglet," said Eeyore, "and then you'll know what we're trying to do."

"I'll take off my tunic and we'll each hold a corner, and then Roo and Tigger can jump into it, and it will be all soft and bouncy for them, and they won't hurt themselves."

"*Getting Tigger down,*" said Eeyore, "and *Not hurting anybody.* Keep those two ideas in your head, Piglet, and you'll be all right."

When Roo understood what he had to do, he was wildly excited, and cried out: "Tigger, Tigger, we're going to jump! Look at me jumping, Tigger! Like flying, my jumping will be. Can Tiggers do it?" And he squeaked out: "I'm coming, Christopher Robin!" and he jumped—straight into the middle of the tunic.

And he was going so fast that he bounced up again almost as high as where he was before—and went on bouncing and saying, "Oo!" for quite a long time—and then at last he stopped and said, "Oo, lovely!" And they put him on the ground.

"Come on, Tigger," he called out. "It's easy."

But Tigger was holding on to the branch and saying to himself: "It's all very well for Jumping Animals like Kangas, but it's quite different for Swimming Animals like Tiggers." And he thought of himself floating on his back down a river, or striking out from one island to another, and he felt that that was really the life for a Tigger.

"Come along," called Christopher Robin. "You'll be all right."

"Just wait a moment," said Tigger nervously. "Small piece of bark in my eye." And he moved slowly along his branch.

"Come on, it's easy!" squeaked Roo. And suddenly Tigger found how easy it was.

"Ow!" he shouted as the tree flew past him.

"Look out!" cried Christopher Robin to the others.

There was a crash, and a tearing noise, and a confused heap of everybody on the ground.

Christopher Robin and Pooh and Piglet picked themselves up first, and then they picked Tigger up, and underneath everybody else was Eeyore.

"Oh, Eeyore!" cried Christopher Robin, "Are you hurt?" And he felt him rather anxiously, and dusted him and helped him to stand up again.

Eeyore said nothing for a long time. And then he said: "Is Tigger there?"

Tigger was there, feeling Bouncy again already.

"Yes," said Christopher Robin. "Tigger's here."

"Well, just thank him for me," said Eeyore.